D0853120

IT HAPPENED AT CAMP PINE TREE

CHOOSE YOUR OWN
NIGHTMARE...

titles in Large-Print Editions:

CHOOSE YOUR OWN

NIGHTMARE... #10

IT HAPPENED AT
CAMP PINE TREE
BY R. A. MONTGOMERY AND
JANET HUBBARD-BROWN

ILLUSTRATED BY BILL SCHMIDT

Gareth Stevens Publishing
MILWAUKEE

For a free color catalog describing Gareth Stevens' list of high-quality books and multimedia programs, call 1-800-542-2595 (USA) or 1-800-461-9120 (Canada). Gareth Stevens Publishing's Fax: (414) 225-0377. See our catalog, too, on the World Wide Web: http://gsinc.com

Library of Congress Cataloging-in-Publication Data

Montgomery, R.A.
    It happened at Camp Pine Tree / by R.A. Montgomery and Janet Hubbard-Brown ; illustrated by Bill Schmidt.
        p. cm. — (Choose your own nightmare; #10)
        Summary: The reader's decisions control the course of a story in which the coolest counselor at Camp Pine Tree has disappeared.
        ISBN 0-8368-1722-2 (lib. bdg.)
        1. Plot-your-own stories. [1. Camps—Fiction. 2. Mystery and detective stories. 3. Plot-your-own stories.] I. Hubbard-Brown, Janet. II. Schmidt, Bill, ill. III. Title. IV. Series.
    PZ7.M7684It   1997
    [Fic]—dc20   96-36060

This edition first published in 1997 by
Gareth Stevens Publishing
1555 North RiverCenter Drive, Suite 201
Milwaukee, Wisconsin 53212 USA

Printed in the United States of America

1 2 3 4 5 6 7 8 9 01 00 99 98 97

IT HAPPENED AT CAMP PINE TREE

You have probably read books where scary things happen to people. Well, in *Choose Your Own Nightmare*, you're right in the middle of the action. The scary things are happening to you!

Summer camp's going to be a major bummer unless Joel, your favorite counselor, shows up. You hope nothing's happened to him. . . .

Fortunately, while you're reading along, you'll have chances to decide what to do. Whenever you make a decision, turn to the page shown. The thrills and chills that happen to you next will depend on your choices.

Go ahead and choose. Joel is waiting. . . .

The rustic WELCOME TO CAMP PINE TREE sign looms large as your father pulls up to the camp's main office. This is your second year at Camp Pine Tree. The camp sits on a beautiful lake and is ringed by tall pine trees. The huge main building, Central Lodge, is directly off the main road, and the cabins and playing fields lie below, toward the lake.

You can't wait to see all your old friends— especially Allie. She was your best friend last summer. The two of you had a great time. One big reason was Joel, the athletics counselor.

Everyone at Camp Pine Tree loves Joel. He's a terrific storyteller, for one thing, and a great sailor and rock climber. And he loves playing jokes. He always freaks out the new campers by cooking grasshoppers over a fire and eating them. He's very cool.

You leap out of the car in your bare feet the second it stops. *Ugh.* Something cold and gooey oozes between your toes. You look down and see a melted chocolate ice-cream cone.

Turn to page 2.

A loud "Ha, ha, ha!" resounds in your ears. You look up and feel the blood rush to your face. Lennie! The counselor everyone hates is back.

Lennie is the camp director's nephew and a real pain. He's the worst counselor at Camp Pine Tree. He has dark, bushy eyebrows, narrow, slitted eyes, and the whitest skin you've ever seen.

Lennie puts his clammy hand on your arm. "So, you've got cold feet about coming back, huh?" he asks. "Ha, ha, ha!"

You jerk away and strut up the lodge steps to the registration desk that has been set up on the huge front porch. Several kids are registering with the secretary, Eleanor. Lennie follows you. Ignoring him, you turn to Eleanor.

"Hi, Eleanor."

"Hello, dear. Glad to see you," she says. "I understand you will be helping out in the office a little this summer?"

Go on to the next page.

"Yes, Allie and I will," you tell her. Mr. Fosgood, the camp director, has asked you and Allie to be helpers this summer. The position will give you a few extra privileges, like avoiding kitchen duty.

"And I hear you'll be part of Lennie's team," Eleanor says.

"What?" you ask, surprised. "I'm supposed to be working with Joel."

Eleanor frowns and fidgets nervously with some camp applications on her desk.

"Joel?" she asks, as if she doesn't know the name. Her voice suddenly sounds high-pitched. "Oh yes, Joel. Well, we really don't know, do we?"

"Don't know what?" you ask.

Before she can answer, Mr. Fosgood comes over. "Someone—I can't say who—was asking after you, about twenty minutes ago." He points toward the cabins. "They went that-away."

"Allie!" you cry. It has to be Allie. But before you can go find her, you've got to help your dad finish unloading your stuff. You race back outside.

Turn to page 4.

4

"Come help unload," your dad calls.

"I'm coming!" you reply.

Hurriedly, you help your mom and dad carry your gear to your cabin. You pick the same bunk as last year. After hugging them good-bye, you run down the path behind Central Lodge. The gate to the dock area is unlocked. You can vaguely make out the shape of someone standing on the bow of Joel's favorite sailboat. No one else was allowed to sail that boat last summer. The figure appears to be motioning to you. Is it Joel?

If you want to see who it is, turn to page 16.

If you'd rather find Allie first, turn to page 50.

You feel worse than ever. "Do they think he's around?"

Lennie nods. "Yep. Maybe we'll see him today," he says mysteriously. "I can't wait to get up there and check on my snake pit. Now get in line for breakfast." He walks away and leaves you standing there alone.

Snake pit?

You join Allie in the food line. Today they're serving pancakes and sausage.

"That Lennie is a total creep," Allie says, as the cook flips three pancakes onto a plate and hands it to her. "I can't believe he's leading the hike. It figures."

You nod and pick up a glass of orange juice. "Don't worry. We'll still have fun," you say. "Maybe we'll find some clue about Joel."

After breakfast, you and Allie go back to your cabins. You spend the morning taking archery lessons with your cabin, while Allie's cabin is at the arts and crafts pavilion. Then, after lunch, everyone who has signed up for the hiking trip meets in front of Central Lodge.

Turn to page 73.

6

"The only other person with a key to the dock is Joel, and he's not around. He's . . ."

"What?" you ask.

"Disappeared," Lennie says. "Five days ago. Gone."

Your mouth drops open.

"It happened on Counselors' Day—you know, when all the counselors get together before the campers arrive? We sailed to Mystery Island for the day." Mystery Island is a small island about twenty miles from camp. It's forbidden to campers.

"I took my uncle's boat, and Joel took his," continues Lennie. "And we raced. But somehow I lost him. And when I came back, his boat was here, but he wasn't. His belongings were gone from his cabin, too. No one has seen him in five days."

"Didn't you call the police?" you ask.

"Sure, my uncle did. But there was no sign of foul play. The police couldn't do anything." Lennie smiles at you. "Joel wasn't that great, anyway."

Turn to page 21.

You decide to head back to the campsite. Allie gets everyone to sing camp songs as you trudge uphill. The forest is shadowy. It's hard to see where you're going. You can't wait to get back to a warm fire and a snack. The camp cook has packed tinfoil dinners for everyone, along with rolls and cookies. Camp rules forbid cooking a meal without a counselor, but this is an emergency.

Up ahead you see the tents. You run up with one of the campers but stop dead in your tracks. Someone has been at the campsite!

Hurry to page 52.

8

"Are you okay?" Allie calls. You see a tiny speck of light above you.

"I think so!" you yell back. "But I don't know how long I can hang on!"

"I'm coming!" she calls.

"Watch out!" you scream. "It's very slippery!" You hold on tightly. The wind blows around you, making soft hissing noises.

After what seems like hours, Allie reaches you. You're exhausted—your arms have never felt so tired. You feel as if you've been hanging on to this tree forever.

Allie flicks on the flashlight. "Okay," she says, "now let me just—*ahhhhhh!*"

Turn to page 63.

As you step through the main entrance of Central Lodge, you are met by a whirling dervish who shrieks your name and grabs you around the neck. Allie! The two of you jump up and down, making a spectacle of yourselves.

Her hair is a bit longer, and her braces are off, but other than that, she looks just the same. She's wearing a striped T-shirt and shorts with little daisies embroidered on them.

"So we're official helpers this year," Allie says, giving you a playful punch on the arm. "Me and you and Joel and the vampire Lennie."

"Shhh," you warn her. "He's been like a shadow since I got here." You pull Allie aside. "Something weird is going on, Allie. Joel's disappeared."

"What!" Allie's mouth drops open in surprise. "What do you mean, disappeared?"

"He's gone. Lennie says he went to Mystery Island on Counselors' Day, and then he just vanished. No one has seen him since."

Turn to page 34.

10

Lennie comes strolling in. He stops. "What—What are you two doing here?" He gasps, then runs over and yanks the brownie out of your hand. "Don't tell me you ate this?" he shrieks.

"Yeah. They did," Joel says abruptly. "What's going on here?"

You grab the side of the table. You're going to pass out. But before you do, you hear the whole thing. Lennie set Joel up. He gave him the wrong starting date. He lied about going sailing with him. He sent all the other counselors on a phony treasure hunt. And he poisoned the food. It won't kill Joel—but it will make him very sick for two to three months. A whole summer.

But you and Allie weigh a lot less than Joel does. The poison hits you much more powerfully.

At least Joel's alive, you think as you drift off to sleep.

The End

12

"Okay, everybody, we all have to work together to get back," you announce. "Follow Allie."

"Thanks a lot," Allie whispers.

"Now," you continue, "I know it's dark, but we only have one flashlight, so no whining." You look pointedly at Penny.

Tanner pulls some matches out of his pocket. "I've got matches!"

Allie gives him a hug. "Matches are against the rules, but good for you." She laughs. "Let's go."

You proceed in single file, going downhill. To your dismay, it starts to drizzle, making the trail really slippery. You only have two hours until it will be pitch-dark.

You hike down for about half a mile, singing the Camp Pine Tree song, which puts everyone in a good mood. The air feels chilly.

Allie stops and looks around. "Does any of this look familiar?" she asks.

"Not really," you whisper.

Turn to page 39.

"So, are you two excited about camp?" Jill asks.

"We'd be more excited if Joel was here," Allie says glumly.

Lennie rolls his eyes. Jill shrugs. "Why don't you go back up to the office and finish helping out with registration?" she suggests. "You can meet us down at the lake at four o'clock for the swim placement tryouts. And the welcome ceremony starts at six."

"Okay," you say, getting up and wiping the grass off your shorts. You and Allie head back to Central Lodge.

Turn to page 22.

14

"I don't know," you say. You hope the other kids don't wake up. The growling grows louder. It sounds like two animals fighting. They bump into the tent!

The counselors have warned you all about rabid animals. Could it be bears?

The kids begin to wake up and cry. You can hear the fighting animals, but you can't see anything. If they get inside the tent, it's all over. A loud squeal and a grunt that sounds inches away make you jump. You've never been this scared.

Then, silence.

Shhh. Turn to page 83.

Allie bolts out the door. You give Mr. Fosgood and Jill a quick smile and rush out after her. Allie is running down the path toward the dock. "Wait!" you yell. She stops and waits for you to catch up, jumping impatiently from one foot to the other.

"Where's the envelope?" Allie asks when you get closer. She grabs your hand. "It was in my pocket, then it wasn't!"

"I didn't see it! Did it fall out in Mr. Fosgood's office?"

"I don't know," Allie says, wringing her hands.

Turn to page 59.

16

You run down the path toward the figure on the sailboat. The sun is in your eyes. You stop, out of breath. No one's there. That's strange. You could have sworn you saw someone. Was it Joel? Or Lennie?

Everything is in perfect order. You stand for a moment and listen to the waves slapping gently against the hull of the small sailboat. Pulling the boat toward you a little, you throw one leg over the side and hop on board. Shielding your eyes with your hand, you turn back toward the dock. You are startled to see Lennie standing there watching you.

Turn to page 41.

"What's that smell?" asks Charlie, a fellow camper. "Yuck."

Jill sticks her head through the cave entrance. "It's starting to drizzle," she says, ignoring Charlie's question. "We'll stay a lot drier here."

You take off your backpack along with the others and pull out your flashlight. "Come on," you say to Allie. "Let's explore." Jill is busy organizing everyone.

Allie leads the way into the cave. She pulls her bandanna up over her nose, and you do the same. It's creepy. A bat swoops down, barely missing your head, then soars away.

The cave is enormous. You bend down to avoid the cobwebs and make your way farther back. It's as silent as a tomb inside. You can't hear the other campers anymore.

Something glints in the flashlight beam. You take Allie's arm and walk over to investigate. It's a pile of animal bones. Both of you start backing up.

"I'm not sleeping here," Allie says. "I don't care what Jill says."

"Me neither," you agree.

Turn to page 24.

18

Rushing back, you take the envelope before she can see *Joel Carpenter* in the upper left-hand corner and *To Mr. Fosgood* on the front, with no address.

"Thank you so much, Eleanor," you gush. "I must have dropped it." You feel bad about lying, but this might be the only way to find Joel.

Allie is waiting for you down the path. She looks panic-stricken. "What'd she say?"

"Eleanor didn't have her glasses. She thought the letter belonged to us!"

"Whew." Allie exhales. "Come on. Let's go down to the lake. We can work out a plan there." You put the folded envelope in your pocket and start walking.

"Do you want to take out a canoe?" Allie asks. "That way we'll be alone. No one will bother us."

"Okay," you say. Since you both were in the highest swimming group last year—the Sailors—you're allowed to take out boats without an older counselor's supervision.

Turn to page 32.

"Come on," whispers Allie, pointing behind you. The two of you try to crawl back a little farther into the cave. You can't think straight, you're so scared. You try to feel your way around with your hands. You can hear Allie's breathing. You try to stand up, but you slip. Your hand lands in something wet and lumpy.

"Allie!" you whisper in a panic. "Shine the light on my hand!"

"I can't," she whispers back. "Whatever is out there will get us."

"I don't care!" you cry. "Help me!"

Turn to page 28.

20

Allie is waiting for you, fully dressed. Mystery Island it is! The two of you race to the sailboat and climb aboard.

"Let's get moving before somebody comes," Allie says.

It's a beautiful day. The wind ripples through your hair, and for a moment you forget you're on a mission. You are convinced that Lennie left Joel on Mystery Island. The island has been off-limits to campers for two years, though no one knows why. Mr. Fosgood is adamant about it. No campers on Mystery Island.

The lake is huge, with eighty miles of shoreline. It will take you a couple of hours to reach the island.

You know you could get into big trouble for this. Mr. Fosgood just bought this boat last year.

"Do you think Lennie would hurt anyone?" Allie asks.

"No," you say. "He's mean, but he's harmless." You pause. "At least I hope so."

Turn to page 40.

You shake your head in disgust. Joel was the best counselor here. But why would he just disappear?

Suddenly being around Lennie is making you nervous. "I'm going back," you say. "I want to see if Allie has arrived." You hop off the boat, avoiding contact with Lennie, and run up the path toward Central Lodge.

Lennie is acting as if Joel ran away. What if something *did* happen to him—what if he was *murdered*? Did he ever really make it back from Mystery Island?

You don't like the sound of this.

Turn to page 9.

22

"I want to get a drink," Allie says, walking toward Mr. Fosgood's office. There's a water fountain in there. You follow her.

"Hey!" says Allie, pointing to Mr. Fosgood's desk. A letter with Joel's return address on the envelope is sitting there.

You hear Mr. Fosgood's voice. "Come on," you plead. "We could get into trouble."

"It may be a clue about Joel!" Allie whispers excitedly. Quickly she stuffs the letter into her shorts pocket.

Turn to page 61.

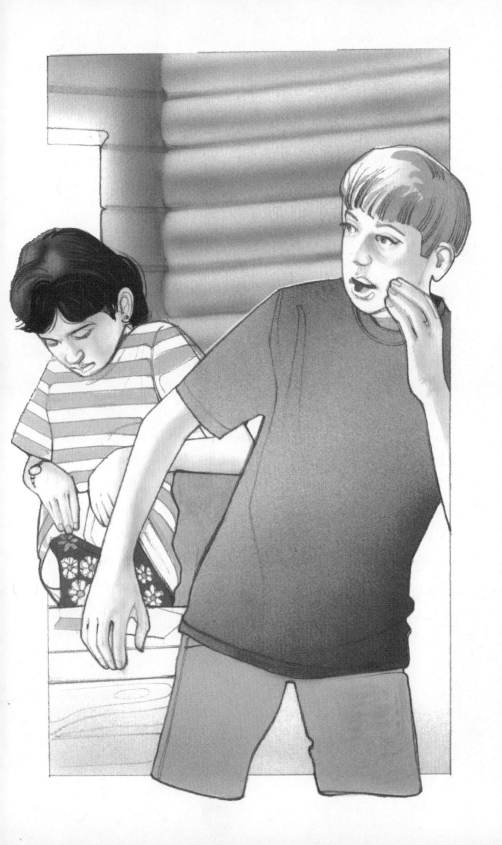

24

You rush back the way you came. Soon you see light coming from the cave entrance. You speed up. When you get to the mouth of the cave, no one is there. "Hey, guys!" you shout. Where did everybody go?

"Do you think they left us on purpose?" you ask.

"Maybe something came after them," Allie says. "But wouldn't they have called for us?"

You begin yelling. "Jill! Help!" Then you turn to Allie. "They can't be far. Let's follow that trail over there. I'm sure we'll catch up."

"I don't know if that's such a good idea," says Allie. "Maybe we should stay here in case they come back."

"With all those bones?" you ask.

"There aren't any out here at the entrance," Allie says. "And at least it's dry. Besides, they'll come back looking for us soon. I'm sure of it."

If you want to stay at the cave, turn to page 78.

If you want to follow the trail, turn to page 54.

"Race you to the dining hall!" Allie says when you knock on her cabin door. The race ends in a tie.

In the dining hall you see a few other campers who have straggled in. Lennie comes rushing over. "Jill and I've got quite a trip planned," he says. "Got your hiking boots?"

"I thought Tom was leading the trip," Allie replies. "Where is he?"

"Sick," Lennie says flatly. "From eating this." He pulls a container out of his backpack and opens it. You nearly gag from the smell of rotting fish.

"That's disgusting," Allie says, holding her nose. "And your jokes suck."

"Have you heard about Joel? He fell into my snake pit and was eaten alive," Lennie says, laughing as Allie walks away, too furious to say anything.

"Come on, Lennie," you say. "You make it sound like you're glad Joel disappeared."

"He's such a show-off, but I don't wish him dead. He sent a letter to my uncle, but it's gone," Lennie says. "Uncle Fosgood called the police."

Turn to page 5.

26

You are close enough now to see Joel without binoculars. The wind has died down and the water is calmer. That's strange, you think. Lennie doesn't seem to be making any effort to get to the island now.

"Hey, Joel!" Allie calls. "It's us!"

"Allie," you say nervously, "look at the water. I've never seen water like this."

Allie looks down. The water is a shiny, greenish yellow color. You suddenly feel uneasy about this whole situation.

You turn around to see where Lennie and Jill went. Their boat looks like a tiny speck in the distance.

"Why did they give up?" you ask Allie.

She shrugs. "Who knows? Come on, let's get Joel!"

"Allie!" you yell. She turns, looking irritated. "What now?" she asks impatiently.

"Look at all the dead fish," you say, pointing to the water. "They're everywhere!"

"Gross!" Allie exclaims. Then she cries, "Watch out for those rocks!"

Turn to page 36.

Allie hesitates, then shines the flashlight on you. Your hand is covered in blood. She gasps. Moving the light down, you see a decaying fox. Maggots are climbing all over the body.

"Ewwwww!" you scream at the top of your lungs. You keep screaming. A light comes toward you. You hear laughter. You feel totally sick. It's a man, wearing shorts and a baseball cap.

Allie gasps. "Joel!"

Is it really him? Find out on page 46.

"Noooo!" A bloodcurdling scream from the path makes you jump. Lennie runs back down the path, with you and Allie right behind him.

Tanner, one of the younger campers, is standing in the middle of the path. He's trembling so hard he can't speak.

Allie gives him water and puts her arm around him. He points into the woods. "I saw two monsters," he gasps. He looks up and sees Lennie laughing. "I'm not joking," he cries.

"I'll go back down there and see if I see anything," Lennie says.

"What are we supposed to do?" you ask.

"Sit and rest," Lennie says. "I'll be right back."

One hour goes by, then two. The sun is low in the sky. Some of the younger kids look scared. You don't want to spend the night here in this swampy area. You glance at your watch. It's 6:30. And no Lennie.

"Should we go look for Lennie?" Allie finally asks.

Decide on page 66.

The flashlight batteries are wearing out. "Hurry," you tell the younger campers. "We don't have much light."

"Let's squish together in the same tent," Allie offers. Soon the sleeping bags are laid out, and you all climb in. You are so tired you fall asleep immediately.

A low growl wakes you. It's coming from outside the tent. You reach over and tap Allie. You can't see her, but you can feel her sit up.

"What is it?" she whispers.

Turn to page 14.

You feel as if you've been walking forever. Suddenly Allie stops. She hops over a tree root and approaches an object hanging from a tree limb. "Hey!" she exclaims. "Isn't this Joel's necklace?"

You run over and retrieve it. It's definitely the smooth round stone Joel always wore.

"Should we keep going?" Allie asks.

You look up at the sky. It's starting to drizzle. "Maybe we should head back to our campsite," you say. "It's a lot closer than the camp. And we only have one flashlight."

If you decide to return to the campsite, turn to page 7.

If you try to return to Camp Pine Tree, turn to page 12.

32

You stop by your cabins to put on your swimsuits and T-shirts and then head down to the lake. It's pretty hot. Being out on the water will be nice. You wave to Kelly, the assistant sailing instructor, who is lining up kids for the swim test. The camp has a special area surrounded by docks for swimming.

"Do you need help?" calls Allie.

"No, everything's under control. Go out and have fun!" Kelly calls back.

You and Allie pick out a canoe. While Allie turns it over, you grab the oars. Then Allie hops in, and you push off and jump in behind her.

The two of you paddle out about fifty yards. You glance around to make sure no one is watching. Kelly and Jill are teaching kids to swim in the shallow end of the docked area. You open the envelope and pull out the letter.

Before you can read a word, a huge hand appears over the rim of the canoe. Allie shrieks. As you reach to knock the hand away, the canoe tilts precariously.

Turn to page 51.

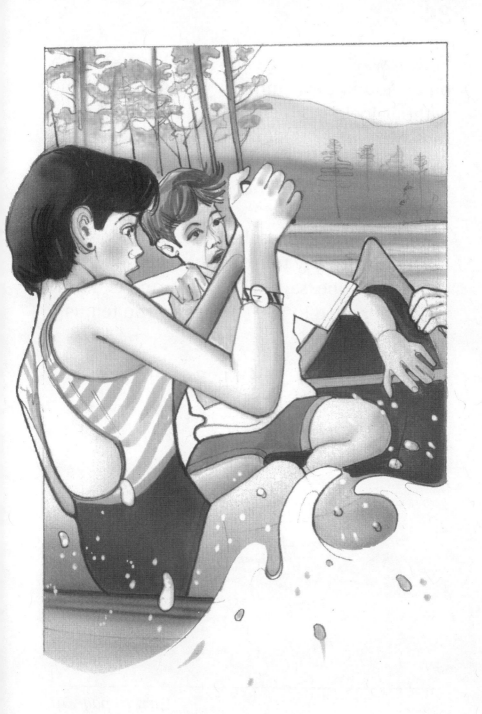

"No way!" Allie gasps. You look at each other. You know camp just won't be the same without Joel. "Let's talk to Mr. Fosgood," Allie says worriedly. "He'll tell us if it's true. People don't just disappear. They either run away or something horrible hap—" She breaks off. "There's Mr. Fosgood!"

Mr. Fosgood approaches you, a clipboard in his hands. "Ready to help?" he asks.

"Okay," Allie says. "But we want to know what happened to Joel. What can you tell us?"

Turn to page 70.

An animal body, that is. You and Allie tiptoe over to it. It's a dead raccoon. You're shocked at how big it is. And how bloody.

"Look! Fresh tracks!" Allie says. "They look human. Come on. If Lennie thinks this a big joke, I'll get him fired."

"We don't have enough light," you say.

"We'll just go a few feet," Allie whispers.

You follow, feeling uncertain. Allie tells you to put the flashlight away. She lights a match. "See, look at these footprints!" she exclaims. "I think they're fresh." The match goes out. While Allie lights another, you move a couple of feet in front of her.

You hear Penny calling your name. "Coming!" you yell. "Let's go back, Allie."

You reach out in the dark to grab Allie's sweatshirt, but she isn't there. "Allie!" you cry.

She's gone!

Hurry to page 77.

The boat is bobbing up and down. There is no wind now. It's so hot you can barely breathe.

"Joel!" you shout again. With great effort, he raises his arm. You know it must be your imagination, but it looks as if he is surrounded by a greenish, phosphorescent light.

"What's wrong with you?" Allie shouts.

"I'm sick!" he cries. "I need help."

Your boat is within a hundred yards of shore now. Suddenly you hear a loud crunch. "Oh no!" you cry. Allie manages to get the boat away from the rocks.

"What's the damage?" she asks.

"Not too bad," you reply. "A tiny hole."

Joel is now wading out into the water. He puts his hand on the boat to steady it.

"Thanks, guys," he says. "I thought I was a goner."

His face is covered with lots of big scabs. And his eyes look red and weak. You are a little frightened. You glance at Allie and see that she's scared, too.

"Wait a second," Allie says slowly. "What's wrong with you?"

Turn to page 56.

You can't leave Joel here. Quickly you inflate your emergency raft. Allie grabs her backpack, which holds a couple of bottles of water, some granola bars, and some apples, and jumps into the raft. You're right behind her. The wind has died down, so rowing is not difficult.

"You're braver than I am," Joel says when you reach shore. "Welcome to Mystery Island."

Neither you nor Allie says anything. You're sure that Joel doesn't know how awful he looks. His skin is peeling off in sheets, and he's lost a lot of hair.

"What're you two staring at?" He smiles.

"You, that's what," Allie says. "Everyone has just about given up on you."

"Was that Lennie sailing behind you?" Joel asks.

"He followed us almost all the way," you reply. "But as we got closer, he turned back."

"Good ole Lennie," Joel says. "He's scared."

Turn to page 57.

You watch as Phyllis, a bubbly counselor you met last year, steps to the middle of the circle. "Now everybody pick a mask," she says. This is one of your favorite Camp Pine Tree traditions. Everyone picks a mask out of a huge box and acts out the character. A big game of hide-and-seek with the masks follows, and then everyone gathers around the fire and feasts on s'mores.

You put your hand into the box Lennie is bringing around and pull out a chicken head. You get up and act like a chicken laying an egg. It feels good to be laughing again. Allie pulls out a monster mask. When it's time for hide-and-seek, you run up a hillside and hide behind a huge boulder.

It is almost dusk. The masks make the game really spooky. You decide to run farther uphill. Panting, you climb a big maple tree. You sit there, waiting for the bell to ring signifying the game is over. Suddenly a shadow moves beneath you. Is it a bear?

Turn to page 45.

The brush gets thicker as you descend. You think you hear water running.

"Water!" you cry out. "Hear it? Last year Joel told us if we ever got lost to try to find water."

The sound of flowing water is getting louder. You shine the flashlight directly ahead. A river! You push through the bushes and find yourself standing on a steep bank.

A couple of campers want to follow the river downstream, but Allie convinces them that it would be dangerous at this time of night. You decide you'll stay where you are tonight and hike downstream tomorrow.

"I see lights on the river," whispers Tanner. A strange light floats toward you. It has a greenish cast.

"We'll get rescued!" Penny cries. She and the others start to stand up. But something about the light disturbs you.

"Wait a minute," you say.

The light gets closer and closer. You dimly make out the outline of a canoe.

Turn to page 75.

40

You notice the wind is changing. Clouds are gathering overhead. It doesn't look good.

"Hope it doesn't get rougher!" Allie shouts, looking a little worried.

While she readjusts the lines, you look back. "Somebody's following us!"

Allie pulls out the binoculars. "It's ole rat-face Lennie," she says. "Act like we don't see him."

You can make out Mystery Island in the distance. Sailing in close will be tricky because of the shallow water and rocks. All you need is Lennie trailing you. He must have been spying.

"He's gaining on us!" Allie yells. "Looks like he wants us to stop."

"He'll just tell us to turn around!" you yell back. "We've gotten this far. Let's go the distance."

Lennie's boat is now almost parallel with yours. Jill is with him. Lennie motions toward the sky with his arm. He's yelling something.

"What's he saying?" you ask.

Turn to page 60.

"Oh!" you exclaim. "You scared me!"

"Really?" Lennie says, his eyes narrowing even further. "What are you doing down here?"

Lennie's attitude annoys you. "I thought I saw somebody waving from the boat," you say.

"Nobody's been down here," Lennie states flatly. "My uncle only gave me the key to the dock area ten minutes ago."

"Well, I saw somebody," you insist.

Turn to page 6.

42

You decide to follow Lennie. "What is this snake pit you keep talking about?" you ask.

He laughs. "Oh, I collect snakes and throw them into this huge pit I dug. Sometimes they kill each other."

"Have you ever been bitten?" Allie asks.

"Once. It was pretty bad."

"I hate snakes," you say. You walk along in silence, wishing now you had gone with Jill. There are ten campers in your group in all, including Allie. Lennie has insisted on going in the opposite direction from Jill's group. You think that's pretty weird.

Lennie stops and looks around. "This will be our campsite," he says. The ground is spongy and uneven. Lennie dumps his enormous backpack and begins setting up two tents. Everyone else does the same.

"Listen up, guys," Lennie says. "I'm going to teach you how to read a map and a compass. Jill and her team are three miles west of us. We'll meet up with them tomorrow and go back to camp together."

Turn to page 29.

"Let me see those again," Allie asks. You hand her the binoculars. You're heading straight for the island.

"It's a person!" Allie shrieks. "Waving his arms around!"

"You sail this thing," you tell Allie. You wish this boat had a motor on it like Lennie's. As you're switching places, the horrible thought occurs to you that Lennie might have to rescue you.

"It's Joel! It has to be!" Allie yells. You grab the binoculars and focus on the island. It *is* Joel! But something is peculiar. You adjust the lenses and look again. Joel looks different.

Lennie notices the figure, too. He is trying to get there first. Joel is now standing still, watching. Lennie is motioning wildly for you to do something, but you don't understand what he's trying to tell you. He finally stops.

Allie suddenly turns to you. "Joel looks really weird!" she yells. "He's almost bald!"

Quick! Turn to page 26.

Your heart is beating fast. You stare down at the shape below. It's not a bear. A tall person wearing a skeleton mask is sitting on the branch below you!

You try to see more closely. The person beneath you suddenly looks up, and the mask drops back.

"Ahhhh!" you scream. The next thing you know, Mr. Fosgood is standing over you. Lots of campers are hovering around.

"Are you all right?" Mr. Fosgood asks, looking concerned.

Turn to page 58.

"Hey there, Allie!" Joel gives her a hug. He looks great: tall, tan, and grinning from ear to ear. "What's going on?"

"We've been so worried!" Allie tells him. "Where were you? What's going on?"

Joel grins. "I wanted to escape the registration days. That's why I showed up late. And when Mr. Fosgood told me you were all up here on an overnight trip, I decided to come up and give you a little welcome-back joke." He slaps you on the back. "Jill and the others are waiting for you outside."

"Oh. So this isn't really a dead fox," you say, sighing with relief.

Joel frowns. "Nope. It is. I only wanted to hide and scare you. I had no idea you'd stick your hand into the guts of a dead animal." He wrinkles his nose, then takes off his shirt and wipes your arm.

"Let's go get you cleaned up," he says, still grinning.

The End

Allie speaks up. "I don't know anything about a document," she says indignantly. "Eleanor left for a few minutes and asked me to answer the telephone."

"It's true," you add.

Mr. Fosgood's forehead is shiny with sweat. He seems to relax a little. "I believe you," he says. "But who would take a letter off my desk?"

You shrug.

"May we go now?" Allie asks. "We're late for swim tryouts."

Mr. Fosgood smiles. "Of course." He and Jill retreat up the path. You turn to follow Allie toward the lake when you are stopped by Eleanor calling from Central Lodge. You whirl back, panicked. You're dead meat now. Eleanor walks briskly toward you.

"Is this envelope yours, dear?" she asks, a little out of breath. "I found it on the floor next to my desk. I don't have my glasses."

Turn to page 18.

You decide you trust Jill a lot more than you do Lennie and join her group. Jill puts a seventy-five-pound backpack on and tells everyone to load up. All the campers are excited.

"I'll give a short course in rock climbing tomorrow if the weather holds," Jill announces as you set out.

"Why did Lennie want to split into two groups?" Allie asks.

"Who knows?" says Jill.

You want to ask her about Joel, but this isn't the time. If only that note hadn't gotten wet. What if Joel needed help?

You keep walking. And thinking.

Your thoughts are interrupted by Allie tapping your arm. "Check out that cave," she says, pointing. You can't believe the size of the opening.

"We'll be spending the night here," Jill tells you. A chill runs up your spine. A horrible smell comes from the cave.

Hold your nose and turn to page 17.

"We'll be back," you promise Joel as you turn the boat and head back to camp.

Allie waves. "Don't worry!" she calls out. "Someone will know what to do!"

Soon Joel and Mystery Island are small dots in the distance. Once you leave the radioactive waters, the wind picks up. There is no sign of Lennie and Jill. You sail without saying anything for an hour. Clouds start to gather, and the wind grows stronger.

Without warning, Allie grabs your arm. "We're leaking," she says. Water is pouring in through the hole made when you hit the rock.

"Start bailing!" you yell.

"It's coming in too fast!" Allie says. She finds a cup and starts tossing water out of the bottom of the boat. The waves are growing bigger by the minute!

Turn to page 69.

50

You race toward Allie's cabin. Her stuff is spread out all over the place. A little note is pinned to her old bunk:

I am hiding and you do not know where. Remember last summer, and glue in your hair?

How could you forget? Allie had been making posters in your cabin and left a bottle of glue propped against your headboard. During the night it turned over and dripped in your hair. You spent the next morning at Central Lodge with Eleanor getting it out.

You dash out the cabin door—and run smack into Lennie.

"Looking for Joel?" he asks.

"No," you say.

"Well, you won't find him," Lennie tells you. "He disappeared five days ago, on Counselors' Day. On a sail to Mystery Island." Mystery Island is about twenty miles away. No one is supposed to go there.

"But—" you start.

Lennie grins. "See ya!" You watch as he runs off. What horrible news! You race up the path to Central Lodge.

Turn to page 9.

A face appears. It's Lennie! He hoists himself up on the side of the canoe.

"Stop!" you scream. "You're going to flip us!"

The next thing you know you're in the water. You clutch the letter with one hand and hold on to the canoe with the other. Lennie is laughing uproariously. You are frantic about the letter.

"Love letter?" he asks you.

He starts swimming back across the lake, leaving you and Allie. Holding the letter out of the water, you finally manage, with Allie's help, to get the canoe upright and climb in. To your horror, you see about fifteen leeches clinging to Allie's skin!

Then you look down and see them on your legs! Gross! You feel sick. Lennie is looking over and pointing, and you see the kids laughing. Some counselor he is!

You and Allie peel the leeches off each other. You peer at the letter. All the ink has blurred. It looks like Joel's handwriting. You can make out the words *Lennie* and *escape*.

Turn to page 65.

52

One tent is smashed in, and the other one is flat on the ground. The backpacks containing your food are gone! Sleeping bags are all over the place. It's dark now, and the only light is your flashlight.

A huge lump forms in your throat. All you can think about is Joel. And, unfortunately, Lennie.

Are they still alive?

"Well," you say, "everything bad that can possibly happen has. Let's set up the tent again and sort out the sleeping bags."

Turn to page 30.

54

You and Allie start heading down the trail. By the time you get back to Camp Pine Tree, it's past dusk. You are both exhausted. All the lights are out except for the ones in the counselors' cabin. As tired as you are, you can't resist peeking in the window.

"I'm going to report Jill for deserting us," Allie says angrily.

"Good," you whisper as you peer inside. You see several big tables heaped with platters of sandwiches, cheese and crackers, and brownies. "Wow!" you say. "That's not fair." You're not allowed to keep food in your cabin.

Allie laughs. "You've got quite a stash, I noticed."

"Just peanut butter and crackers," you say huffily. "Which reminds me. I'm starving."

"No way!" says Allie, punching your arm.

"What's your problem?" you ask, annoyed. "Wh—"

"Look!" Allie exclaims. Joel has just walked into the room! He helps himself to a sandwich and a can of root beer. You and Allie stare through the window and then at each other. What does this mean?

Turn to page 71.

Mr. Fosgood shrugs. "What can I do? All I know is Joel's not here—and camp must go on." He walks away.

You go back to the registration desk on the front porch. By now hundreds of kids and parents are milling around. It seems as if everyone is carrying a sleeping bag, suitcase, or backpack. In minutes you and Allie are collecting forms and making sure that campers have all the required gear, like bug spray and sleeping bags. One of the counselors brings out sandwiches for all the workers.

After a couple of hours, Mr. Fosgood comes over to your table. "Lennie's organizing a welcome-back volleyball game out back," he says. "Why don't you two join him?" He turns to walk away. Allie grabs his arm.

"Mr. Fosgood? I can't work with Lennie."

Mr. Fosgood's face reddens. Allie speaks up before he has a chance to say anything. "Last year he caused a lot of trouble. He swore he'd get Joel fired this summer. He's so jealous."

Turn to page 64.

"Lennie talked me into sailing over here in our Sunfish," he explains. "My boat overturned, and I realized too late that there was something wrong with the water here. The water that surrounds Mystery Island is . . . radioactive."

"That's what Lennie was yelling—*radioactive!*" cries Allie.

"Why didn't Lennie help you?" you ask.

"He told me he'd go for help," Joel says. "But it's been a long time. At least four days."

"What a coward!" you cry. "He told everybody you'd disappeared!"

You look at Joel and feel sick inside. Joel smiles sadly. "Go on back. You shouldn't be near me. Go get help," he says softly.

"We can rescue you, I know we can," Allie insists. "If you sit at that end of the boat and don't touch us, it'll probably be okay."

Turn to page 67.

"They could charge him with murder for leaving you like this and not telling anyone," you say.

"It's been a nightmare," Joel says.

"We have some food," you tell him. "That should make you feel better." You make sure not to touch him.

Joel leads you back to his campsite. Allie pulls out a water bottle and an apple. Joel eats as if he's starving. You and Allie wait silently.

"Let's get going," Allie says. "This place is creepy." Looking around, you realize that practically everything on the island is dead.

"Yeah. I need to get to a hospital," Joel says.

You walk back to the lakeshore. You feel incredibly relieved. Even though the situation is terrible, you'll soon be back at Camp Pine Tree.

But when you get to shore, you're in shock. The inflatable raft has shriveled up. There's practically nothing left of it!

Turn to page 82.

"I think so." You realize you must have fallen out of the tree. Allie comes running over.

"I think you should go to the infirmary and let Ms. Huff check you out," Mr. Fosgood says. "Allie, you go, too. Okay everybody, time for s'mores."

Your head really hurts. "Did you slip?" Allie whispers.

"I think I saw Joel," you reply. "Wearing a skeleton mask."

Allie is doubtful. "That new counselor, Tom, looks like Joel. Maybe . . ."

"He's around here somewhere, I know it!" you say. "Maybe Mystery Island? That's where he was on the day he disappeared. Do you want to go there tomorrow?"

Turn to page 68.

Suddenly you hear shouting. Mr. Fosgood and Jill are marching toward you. The expressions on their faces are grim.

"I'm missing an important document," Mr. Fosgood says through clenched teeth. "It was on my desk an hour ago."

Your father has told you that lying is okay only in life-threatening situations. Is Joel's life at stake?

*If you want to confess,
turn to page 74.*

*If you decide it's important enough to lie,
turn to page 47.*

"Who knows? He's probably trying to tell us it's going to storm."

"Maybe we should go back," you say. "Neither of us is that great a sailor. If only we knew for sure that Joel was on the island . . ."

"This is our only chance to look for him!" Allie shouts.

Lennie looks angry now.

"The . . . radio . . . no . . . rain!" he shrieks. You can't make out a complete sentence. Allie reaches over and turns up the boom box she brought along.

"Can't hear you!" she yells over to Lennie.

"Maybe we should turn around," you say worriedly.

"Wait!" Allie shouts. "Something's moving over there on the island."

You take the binoculars and look. "It's a blue heron, silly," you say.

Lennie turns his motor off. You focus the binoculars on him and Jill. They aren't paying attention to you now. They're looking in the direction of Mystery Island.

Turn to page 43.

When Mr. Fosgood enters, Allie pretends to be speaking on the telephone. "Thank you for calling Camp Pine Tree. I'll have the information sent to you," she says in a businesslike voice. What an actress.

Mr. Fosgood is impressed. "Thank you for taking that call, Allie. Where's Eleanor?"

You notice the letter bulging out of Allie's pocket. "I don't know," Allie replies nonchalantly. "She should be back in a minute." She leans down to tie her sneaker.

"Come on, Allie," you say. "Time for the swim tryouts."

"One more thing," Mr. Fosgood adds. "Don't worry about Joel. I'm doing everything I can to locate him. It's really not your concern. Do you understand?"

Allie nods and turns to leave. Just then Jill comes in.

Turn to page 15.

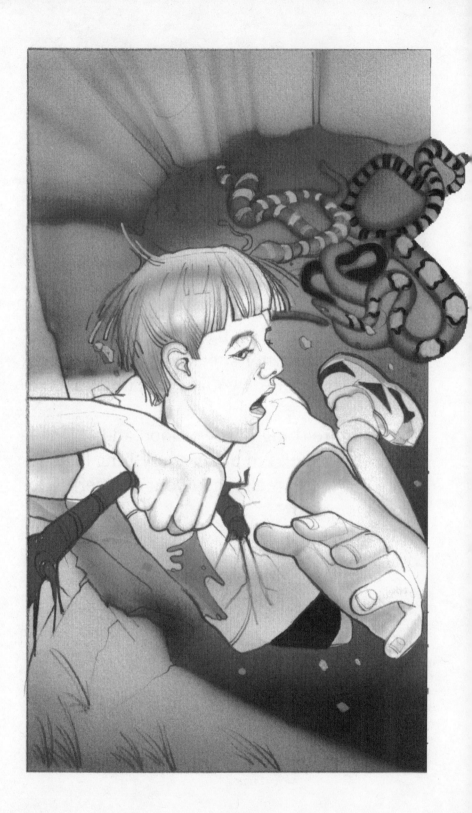

You look down. In the dim light of Allie's flashlight you see movement below you. You try to focus.

"Ahhhh!" you scream at the top of your lungs, clutching the branch harder than ever. You are dangling over Lennie's snake pit! If you hadn't caught the branch, you would be dead!

"Don't worry," Allie gasps. "I'll get help." The light still shines on the slimy, writhing forms beneath you. A bright yellow object in the pit catches your eye. It's a Camp Pine Tree baseball hat. Only one person wore that hat: Joel.

All you can hear is the beating of your heart. And the hissing of snakes.

The End

Mr. Fosgood speaks softly, but his tone is firm. "Last summer was Lennie's first year at camp. Give him another chance." He motions toward Lennie. "Now, I think you'd better get started."

About twenty kids are standing on the grass next to Central Lodge, watching you. You and Allie have no choice but to run over and join them. Lennie is trying to put up a volleyball net. He's having a hard time.

The three of you get the net up, and the game gets under way. You and Allie sit on the grass. You watch as a short, dark-haired girl about sixteen years old comes over to Lennie. She's wearing a Camp Pine Tree polo shirt and shorts. After a few minutes they walk over to you.

"You two are *my* helpers now," Lennie says in his whiny voice. "I know you'd rather help Joel, but since he isn't here, you've got Jill and me."

Jill walks over and sticks out her hand. "Hi," she says.

"Hi," you say back.

Turn to page 13.

Now you're really worried. What if Mr. Fosgood hadn't read the letter? Now he won't be able to help at all. You look up and see tears in Allie's eyes.

"What are we going to do?" you ask. Then you hear Kelly calling from across the lake for you to come in for the ceremony. You and Allie paddle back and join the other campers. The wet letter is balled up in your pocket. You go and change into dry clothes and meet Allie in front of your cabin.

"Maybe we should sneak off and sail to Mystery Island," Allie whispers as you walk toward the ceremony. You don't have time to answer, as all the campers are already sitting around a big bonfire introducing themselves. You join in. Mr. Fosgood gives a little talk and introduces the counselors.

You feel pretty depressed. It doesn't seem right that Joel isn't here.

Turn to page 38.

66

You are scared but don't want to admit it. Since you two are the oldest, you're in charge. But you don't know what to do.

"We have one or two hours of daylight left," you think out loud. "We could probably make it back to camp. But I don't know for sure."

"Let's go back to Camp Pine Tree," one of the kids whimpers.

"Where do you think Lennie is?" asks Penny, a small, curly-haired girl. "Do you think the monsters got him?"

"No," you say. "But that's not a bad idea." Everyone laughs.

Allie hasn't said anything in a long time. It's beginning to get dark.

"Let's head back to camp," Allie finally suggests. "We can leave our stuff here. It's too heavy to carry. Tomorrow we can come back and get it with one of the counselors."

With Allie in the lead, you all head down the path toward Camp Pine Tree.

Turn to page 31.

"I don't want you to take such a terrible risk," Joel states emphatically.

You can see that Joel's condition is worsening. He might not live much longer.

If you want to stay and rescue Joel,
turn to page 37.

If you decide to leave him and get help,
turn to page 49.

68

Allie yawns. "All I want to do is finish unpacking and go to bed. It's late," she adds. "Let's decide tomorrow." The two of you say good night and head for your cabins.

The sun coming through the window next to your bunk wakes you up the next morning. You glance at your watch. It's early. You climb out of your bunk, throw on a T-shirt and shorts, and race over to Allie's cabin.

If you want to go hiking,
turn to page 25.

If you want to go to Mystery Island,
turn to page 20.

It takes all your energy to sail the boat. You've never sailed in a storm before. You think Camp Pine Tree is fairly close, but you can't be sure. Allie keeps bailing.

In the distance, you pick out some head-lights. "It looks like a big boat!" you shout over the roar of the wind.

"Let's go!" Allie screams.

Turn to page 72.

"I'm sorry, but I don't know anything," Mr. Fosgood says. "We're calling everyone we can think of to try and learn of any possible reason he would leave camp so suddenly. I never even saw him. In the meantime, we're replacing him with a new counselor—Jill Johnson."

"Oh," Allie says disappointedly. "But . . ."

Mr. Fosgood waits, looking slightly impatient. "But what, Allie?"

"We—we really miss Joel," Allie says miserably.

"Yeah. He was the best," you add.

Turn to page 55.

You're not about to wait to find out. "Joel!" you scream, rushing into the room and flinging your arms around him. "You're alive!"

He laughs and hugs you back. "Of course I'm alive. What's wrong with you two?"

"We were so worried. We couldn't believe you weren't going to be here this year!" Allie says. "And you missed the opening ceremonies!" You and Allie each grab a brownie and munch ravenously.

Joel frowns. "What are you talking about? Camp starts tomorrow, guys. I'm not late. That's what all this food is here for. For the counselors' welcome-back party." He takes a big bite of his sandwich. "Funny, though. I can't figure out why I'm the only one here."

"No! You're wrong," you say. "The first . . ." You drift off and wipe your forehead. Suddenly you're feeling rather strange.

Allie holds her stomach. "I . . . I'm not feeling well," she moans.

Just then the door bangs open.

Who is it? Turn to page 10.

You sail the boat toward the lights. But you don't seem to get any closer. Exhaustion begins to set in.

"The lights. The lights are closer now!" Allie gasps. "We've got to make it!"

Finally you are close enough to pull alongside the other boat. The wind subsides a little.

"Do you think we'll get in trouble for leaving the sailboat?" you ask, hopping aboard the bigger boat.

"Are you kidding?" Allie asks. "We're in a life-or-death situation!" Her footing gives way as she boards. She struggles upward. One of her legs slips beneath the water.

You grab her arm. "Be careful!"

"I'm fine," Allie says, brushing the water off her leg. "We've got to find the captain."

You race up a short flight of stairs. "Wow!" Allie exclaims behind you. "This is some luxury yacht."

"I feel like we're being watched," you say nervously.

"Hello! Anybody here?" Allie calls.

Turn to page 76.

"Does everyone have their gear? Backpacks? Water bottles?" Jill asks. You all nod.

After leading everyone up the path from camp for about three miles, Jill and Lennie stop. Lennie says he's going to divide the group into two. "Get in this line if you want to be in Jill's group and over here if you want to follow me," he yells.

Even though you hate Lennie, you're unsure about which group to join. What if Lennie really does have a lead on Joel's whereabouts? On the other hand, what if he's bluffing and just planning on causing trouble?

If you want to follow Lennie, turn to page 42.

If you want to follow Jill, turn to page 48.

74

Allie stands as tall as she can. "I saw Joel's return address on an envelope on your desk and I took it."

"I know you did, because I saw you drop it," Mr. Fosgood says angrily.

"Joel was the best counselor here," Allie bursts out. "And he's disappeared and nobody seems to know anything, or even care! I think something fishy is going on."

"And Lennie probably did it," you mutter.

Mr. Fosgood looks at you hard. "For your information, Joel is in Denver. He went out on a vision quest—without telling us. He ended up quitting and heading for Denver. His father just called."

Allie looks distressed. "I thought Lennie . . ."

Mr. Fosgood's expression grows sad. "I regret to have to tell you two that I must call your parents. You have violated a very important rule at our camp: no stealing. We'll have to decide whether you can stay here or not this summer. I'm sorry."

The End

The canoe is almost in front of you. You can't see anybody in it.

Allie shines her flashlight toward the water. The light catches the reflection of silver metal.

You can't believe your eyes.

A skeleton is sitting upright in the middle of the canoe, dressed in a camp sweatshirt and cap.

Believe it on page 80.

You enter a dining room where four places are set. Fine china and silverware grace the table. But there are no people.

You spot a telephone on the wall. "I'll call 911," Allie tells you. But when she picks it up, there's no dial tone.

You and Allie run back outside and look around. No captain. And no land in sight. But gross! The water is now the same disgusting neon green as the water at Mystery Island. The radioactive water! Have you backtracked somehow?

You enter the captain's quarters. The room is full of equipment. You don't see a phone.

"Hello. Welcome to *Eternity*," says a male voice. You spin around. It's Joel! Or at least his skeleton. He holds up his bony hands. He looks even worse than when you saw him earlier.

"How did you get here?" you gasp.

The expression on Joel's face changes. "This ship picked me up after you left," he says. "I look pretty strange, huh? The water ate through to my bones."

Turn to page 84.

"I'm over here," Allie says impatiently. "I can't get these matches to light."

You follow the sound of her voice. To your horror, you lose your balance. The next thing you know, you're sliding down the hill on your butt! You grab a tree root, jerking yourself to a stop.

"Allie!" you scream. You can't find the ground under your feet. You hang on tightly and kick. You're hanging off a cliff!

Hang on until page 8.

You agree to stay put. "It stinks here," you complain.

Allie laughs. "You can say that again. I think it's bear smell. They probably live here during the winter."

"Maybe year-round," you say.

You shine your flashlight around. Spiders, bats, bones, and no telling what else.

Leaning against a stone directly inside the cave, you huddle together and try to rest. It has been an exhausting two days.

"We have to tell Mr. Fosgood about the letter we stole," you say quietly. "Maybe it was really important." You feel like crying. "Joel may have written down exactly where he was going. And we screwed it up!"

"I know," Allie says. She looks miserable. "We'll hike back to camp tomorrow and tell them about the letter. Poor Joel."

Just then a couple of rocks drop from the top of the cave. Is someone up there? Allie reaches over and grabs your hand. Another rock drops. Has someone been standing on top of the cave listening to you?

Find out on page 19.

Your whole body begins to shake. In speech-less horror, you, Allie, and the other campers watch as the skeleton-manned canoe floats downriver in the moonlight. For a few moments, no one says anything.

"We're not staying here tonight," Allie states flatly, grabbing your hand.

"Ditto," you say, your voice trembling. "Let's start walking."

"Wait!" whispers Tanner, pointing. The moon is shining brighter now, and the canoe has turned around. It's heading back toward you.

You stare as the skeleton lifts up a bony hand and waves.

The brim of the cap reads JOEL.

The End

You don't know what to do. Then you notice that the same thing is happening to her hand.

The hand that she used to brush the water off her leg.

In horror, you look at the spot where she grabbed your arm. It's beginning to glow. A pale lime green.

The End

82

"The water!" you shriek. "It must have made the raft decompose!" You swallow. "At least the boat is anchored." But you don't see it. All you can see is a pointed object sticking straight up. It looks like the top of a sailboat.

"Where's the boat?" Allie asks worriedly.

All at once you remember the hole in the boat. Surely that wouldn't have sunk it so quickly!

Your heart sinks, too. Are you doomed to stay on this island forever? Will Lennie let anyone know what has happened?

The three of you stand silently looking out over the poisoned water.

The End

"Somebody has to go outside and check out what happened," Allie says.

"Maybe we should wait until daylight," you say.

"I'm not chicken," Allie says. "I need light, though. Check through all your pockets," she tells the kids.

Penny stops crying long enough to say, "I have some matches."

"Why didn't you tell us before?" Allie asks, frustrated.

"No one asked," Penny blubbers.

Allie unzips the tent flap, lights a match, and steps out. You climb out behind her. You can't see a thing, not even the outlines of trees. A breeze blows out the match. Allie lights another one and begins walking slowly forward. You follow, your heart in your throat. Your flashlight is still attached to your belt. You pull it out and try it again. It works! But it's still quite dim. You shine it near the tent. Oh no! A body is resting against the tent!

Turn to page 35.

"The . . . the radioactive water?" you whisper.

"This is freaking me out!" Allie cries.

"Come and have something to eat," Joel says. "I'll be in the dining room." You watch him leave.

"This is awful! I can't stand to see Joel like this!" Allie says under her breath. "Let's try to escape."

"How?" you ask, practically in tears.

The two of you hurry outside and look over the railing. Dead fish are floating everywhere. The water really smells.

"Oww!" Allie gasps, jumping back.

"What is it?" you cry.

"My leg!"

You look where she's pointing. The skin is beginning to peel off her calf and thigh, right in front of your eyes. The flesh underneath is a pale lime green.

"I'm—I'm radioactive!" she screams, grabbing your arm.

Hurry to page 81.